GATES OF WONDER

FIVE ORIGINAL STORIES OF THE AGENTS OF BIS

STEPHANNIE TALLENT

First e-Book edition March 2021

Ebook ISBN: 978-1-942655-15-2
Print ISBN: 978-1-942655-16-9

www.stephannietallent.com

For Dave

CONTENTS

INTRODUCTION

I've always been a voracious reader. As a young child, I worked my way through the small school library, gathering a galaxy of gold stars for number of books read.

No genre was off limits.

Does anyone remember a story about kittens with wings? Because I know I read something like that.

Elementary school, junior high, high school...the libraries grew larger.

...from Farley and the Black Stallion, to Marguerite Henry and all those wonderful, glorious horses...

...to the intricacies of Agatha Christie, as I worked my way through my mom's bookshelves, full of old paperbacks...I think my mom owned every book by Agatha Christie.

...oh, all of Madeleine L'Engle, all of it...I wanted to be Meg Murry.

...to the complexity of Thomas Covenant (in retrospect, was that really appropriate for a twelve year old? didn't matter—I read them all anyways)...

...to the Cold War spy novels of Helen MacInnes, Robert Ludlum,

Ken Follett, and John le Carre—is it any wonder I ended up as a Military Intelligence officer?

And of course that pattern continues now. If you're thinking I'm a genre omnivore, I'll happily admit to that.

And that's informed my writing.

And especially, this collection.

By creating the Bureau of Interworld Stabilization, I've created a world that I can play in, with multiple genres. I don't have to limit myself to just one genre. I get to have my cake and eat it, too!

Fantasy? Science Fiction? Boom. I can have a world more technologically advanced than ours. I can have one so far away, magic works.

And even mundane worlds harbor adventure and mystery.

Any sort of world I can dream up, I can have a Gate Keeper link to it.

And if I don't have a Keeper handy? Well, Wild Gates pop up. All those stories of the Sidhe or Faeries. Alien abductions. Shoot, the freakin' Bermuda Triangle.

I can have factions within a government agency. Corruption. Spying. I get to explore what happens this side of the Gate, not just what happens *through* the Gate. And...maybe Prime isn't the only world that has people who can manipulate the Gates. Maybe Prime *isn't* Prime. Isn't on top. Chew on that, BIS Director Jason Osaka.

And the characters! I can have newbie Field Agents. Old jaded ones. Gate Keepers who are a bit creepy. People who are satisfied to work behind the scenes...but discover terrible things.

Anything I can dream up, I can make it a part of this world.

Sound fun?

I thought so.

Take my hand.

Come Gate with me.

THE CRY OF THE COYOTE

Sadie tugged on her heavy leather boots and cinched the laces tight, the squeak of the new leather echoing off the bare white walls of the prep room.

No windows, epoxied walls, overhead lights and ultraviolet emitters encased in waterproof housing: the room was optimized to be blasted clean.

Hopping to her feet, she mentally ran through the pre-mission checklist.

Her *first* mission. Her stomach roiled, and not just from the solution of bleach and other antimicrobials used to scrub the room before and after each trip through the gate.

She held back a sneeze. It was a smell she'd figured she'd get used to, when she enlisted for service at the Bureau of Interworld Stabilization, or BIS.

At some point.

She hadn't. It still tickled her nose.

Back to the checklist.

Utility belt with sheathed pocket knife; compass; multi-tool; and forty feet of polypropylene emergency cord, tied in a neat figure eight. Check.

Black canvas backpack stuffed with two days of dehydrated field rations; a lightweight poncho/blanket; basic first aid kit including sunscreen; and water filter. She tucked a pair of thin leather and mesh gloves into one of the outer pockets. Check.

Second canvas and Cordura pack, pre-packed by the Logistics Department, specific for this mission. Check.

Synced watch, firmly strapped to her wrist. Check.

Filled water pack. Check.

Butterflies in stomach, despite popping the anti-nausea meds two hours prior? Check.

Alpha Six Delta, A6D, the target of today's mission, was fully catalogued, with a biome 95.98% the same as Earth Prime, closer than so many other worlds. So close that when something went wrong *there*, it always echoed into Prime. Her world.

The number two rule at BIS was *bring nothing* not *biologically inert to another world*.

Well, as much as was physically possible. You couldn't rid your gut of every bacteria. Or mites living on your eyelashes. But stray viruses hitching a ride on your clothes or skin? Yeah, those got zapped.

Hence the autoclaved clothes, put on once you scoured your hair and body squeaky clean, to be followed by an ultraviolet bath, just before you gated.

If something with awry, if you left *something* behind, you risked a feedback loop. Rumor had it that's what caused the flu pandemic in the nineteen-teens, back before BIS even existed as such, when gating was first discovered.

And the number one rule? *Don't bring anything biologically viable* back. Because the repercussions of that....

Sadie's stomach clenched. So much could go wrong...one of her classes was History of the Bureau of Interworld Stabilization, aka *Past Fuck-Ups*.

The windowless door behind her, leading to the main labs of BIS, swooshed open, as she braided her hair into a single long plait. She glanced nervously at the door opposite.

The door to the transit room that contained the gate.

"You'll do fine, kiddo," said Dr Richards as he followed her glance. Her advisor was already suited up in sturdy khaki canvas trousers, a long sleeved pale sage green work shirt, and a floppy brimmed hat. Typical field uniform. Sadie's matched, except her shirt was still trainee-tan.

Dr Richard's dark craggy face was kind, his warm brown eyes encouraging. "You've trained for two years. You're ready. First trip through is always nerve wracking."

She'd worked her butt off for this chance. A two year track of study and training at BIS, on top of her undergrad degree in Comparative Zoology and a Masters in Public Health. Passed all the genetic tests, verifying she was one of the .005% even capable of passing through a gate sane and in one whole piece. Trained physically until she could have competed as a professional triathlete or mixed martial arts fighter. Completed military survival courses side by side with elite forces.

She *was* ready. And this first mission was straightforward. Two days to drop off bait, containing an oral rabies vaccine, in the Santa Monica Mountains, just to the north of Los Angeles.

The local coyote population in Alpha Six Delta had a rabies break out—or at least the A6D version of the deadly disease.

Los Angeles-A6D was a small farming town, not the metropolis it was in Prime. The disease was likely to be self-limiting in Alpha Six Delta. But an echo could cause a huge outbreak in Prime, where thousands of people hiked in the mountains, and so many homes abutted the range.

Limiting the outbreak made sense.

Fancy homes, Sadie thought uncharitably. Well, something had to fund the BIS budget. She twisted a band around the tip of her braid.

"I'm more than ready," she said. "Let's go."

~

THE GATE DIDN'T LOOK like much. And if you weren't blessed with the genes to perceive it, you wouldn't even see the dark shimmer in the air, even with the stark white lights of the transit room.

A Gate Keeper sat cross-legged on the polished marble floor. Dressed in a simple heathered gray cotton robe, she didn't seem to feel the chill of the room. Her thin hands sculpted the air, swimming through currents only she could see, her narrow face intent.

Jessica.

Sadie knew who all the gate keepers were; all her fellow trainees did.

Someone knew someone who knew someone who'd heard that a BIS agent in the Budapest office (or was it the Munich office? Or London? Sao Paulo? Tokyo?) disappeared after breaking the heart of a keeper.

Never showed up at their destination. Never returned to Prime.

No one wanted to get on the wrong side of a Keeper.

Regardless, the Keepers kept to themselves, spending their off-duty days meditating and practicing memory games. Knowing, deep in their bones, everything they could about a handful of worlds.

That knowledge let them link a gate to its destination.

Let agents like Dr. Richardson and, soon, Sadie, reach the correct world safely.

Sadie wasn't sure if new worlds were discovered by the Keepers, tweaking their expectations and finding what matched, or actually *created* in that moment, when a Keeper imagined it.

Jessica was nice. Some of the Keepers weren't, acting superior to everyone. Snooty jerks. Jessica, however, had lectured to Sadie's class during the first month at BIS, an overview of gate Keepers and an offhand attempt at recruiting. She'd answered their questions with good humor. A couple of Sadie's classmates expressed interest in becoming Keepers, but only one was still in training.

Rumor had it he was going to wash out.

Not many made it.

Sadie had no interest in gate keeping, except as much as she felt she needed to know to actually traverse a gate. She wanted to visit those worlds, not just observe them from a safe distance. Breathe in air from another world. Watch sunsets she couldn't see on Prime. Taste fruit that had no analogue here.

Just a couple minutes more, and she'd be in the Alpha Six Delta. The first of many worlds.

"One minute," whispered Jessica, her voice surprisingly deep. The gate, now an opaque sheet of black glitter, stretching from floor to ceiling, wavered in response to her voice.

"Approach."

The gate would drop them near a fire road near Temescal Peak. They would hike a big loop, dropping off the bait, and return to the fire road gate in thirty six hours. Jessica would open the gate every hour, on the hour, after that, for up to two days for this class of mission, until they returned.

Easy peasy.

"Thirty seconds."

Dr Richards reached for her hand. Sadie clasped his hand firmly. She hoped her hand didn't feel clammy. His hand was dry, rough calluses scraping against her palm.

"Three, two, one—safe gating, my friends—"

Jessica's deep voice faded as they stepped into that starry blackness.

SAGE AND BUCKWHEAT and warm sunlight on her skin and not even a hint of chemicals or smog! Bees buzzed and jays chattered and the world sang to her. Sadie yanked free of Dr. Richards and spun, arms outstretched, giggling, tripping over the rain carved ruts in the fire road and catching herself without thinking.

She loved it, she loved this world, this world of pure sparkling sunlight and brilliant cerulean skies and balmy sea-kissed breezes and rabid coyotes and soaring condors and the earth rumbling unsettled beneath her boots.

"Gate euphoria," Dr. Richards said. "Focus, Sadie. When is an agent most vulnerable? Just after gating."

Disorientation. Nausea. Euphoria. No agent gated without suffering one of those side effects.

"Euphoria is the most dangerous side effect of gating," Dr. Janet Hill, her voice light and amused, lectured. "An agent who's disorientated can ground themselves quickly in the current world. Nausea, well, it sucks, but it passes, usually without the agent actually vomiting. And the anti-emetics you take beforehand are quite effective in preventing the gate gurgies.

"But, euphoria? Think of it like getting narc'd SCUBA diving. You're so happy you don't care if rampaging grizzly is, um, bearing down on you. He's just so pretty, with his fur all shiny in the sun. Til he kills you."

"Kills me," Sadie said. She laughed. Oh, that puffy cloud! It looked like a grizzly bear!

"Snap out of it, kiddo." Dr. Richards, so far away, so very far away. Strain in his patient voice.

"Okay, people, this is the only time you get to legally take drugs during training. And don't think you can go have fun over the next couple weeks. Our drug tests can differentiate between what I'm handing out now, and what you might try recreationally. And the latter will get you booted out." Dr. Hill doled out two lilac-colored capsules to each student. "Over the next week I'll be training you to control euphoria, in case one or more of you is unlucky enough to suffer from it. Now, take one capsule.

"What's the first thing to do with euphoria?" Dr. Hill asked after a couple minutes.

"Breathe," Sadie said. She stopped twirling, and focused on the earth, now quiet, under her feet. Solid. Unmoving. Still.

Breathe in, breathe out.

Sadie hadn't seen Dr. Hill since that week of drug-induced haze. But she would never forget her.

Breathe.

"That's right," Dr. Richards said. "Next?"

"It's like dealing with a panic attack," Dr. Hill commented. "You need a ritual to fall back upon. Find what works for you. And practice it, til it's more natural than breathing—" Her voiced faded away.

"Count down," said Sadie. "Three, two, one—" With each number, she pulled *in*, centering herself. *Blast off!* And she was back to herself.

The sky was still pure unpolluted blue, the clouds puffy with the threat of late summer thunderstorms, and the bees still buzzed around the purple sage, but she could *think*.

Inability to control gate euphoria was a career killer. Oh, there were plenty of jobs at BIS that didn't involve gating. But nothing she wanted to do. And, unfair or not, an agent derailed by euphoria was never treated like someone who chose another of those jobs from the get-go.

"Kiddo?"

"I'm okay. I'm here. Oh gosh, I didn't expect that." Sadie shivered. Thank god for Dr. Hill and those little purple pills.

"It's your first gate," Dr. Richards said, his voice noncommittal.

Some people "outgrew" gate euphoria. They were eligible for key missions, solo missions. Like any other normal agent.

Some didn't outgrow it.

Well, she was here, in Alpha Six Delta, *now*. With a job to do. And until they finished this mission, and gated home, and then she gated on *another* mission, and another after that, she'd have no idea which camp she fell into.

"I'm fine, Dr. Richards," she said. "Let's go."

THEY HIKED about fifteen miles that first day, emptying Dr. Richard's pack of the vaccine-impregnated meat squares. Tomorrow they'd distribute the remainder that Sadie carried.

"They look like granola bars made of beef jerky," she commented. "I've read about them for controlling rabies in various states, but it's the first time I've worked with them."

"First time using them here," Dr. Richards said. "So this mission has two goals. Distribute these, then later monitor and see if they even work to prevent infection. Take that side trail."

Sadie turned down the narrow trail to the right. She heard the gurgle of water ahead, past the large granite boulders studding the trail. Live oaks branched overhead; she took care to avoid the poison oak crowding the rocky trail. The air smelled damp, mineral and tangy.

"Just a little further."

She nodded, focusing on the increasingly steep downhill trail. Just her luck to twist an ankle. She threaded her way between two towering boulders, then gasped.

A fairy pool, glimmering in the shade of the trees, tucked between more boulders, greeted her. Rays of sunlight glittered across its surface. A creek trickled at the far end. "It's so pretty!"

"Thought you'd like it," said Dr. Richards. "We can't camp right by it, too many mosquitoes later, but we can filter water and refill our packs. Wash off our faces."

"Soak our sore feet?" asked Sadie. She didn't have blisters, not yet, but a spot on the ball of her left foot burned.

"Go ahead." He smiled. "I might even join you."

She took off her boots and rolled up her pant legs. The bottom of the pool was sandy, the water clear enough that she could see her toes, even in the shade of the oaks. She sighed in contentment. This. This is what she worked for. To experience all of this, this gorgeous different world, that only a handful of people from her own world had visited. Well, less than a hundred. Probably. Alpha Six Delta was well studied.

Who cared. She was here!

She wouldn't let anything, not euphoria, not *anything*, stop her.

THE LATE SPRING weather was mild enough they just wrapped up in their space blankets to sleep, leaving everything on except their boots. Clothes stiff with sweat? She'd shower back in Prime.

Between the excitement of her first mission, and the physical exertion of hiking up and down hills, Sadie fell asleep as soon as they cleaned up after their meal of rehydrated noodles and peanut butter sauce.

A yip-yipping cry woke her up. The crescent moon had long set, and the scattering of stars did little to light the clearing. But she could see well enough to tell she was alone.

She felt for her boots, smacking each one against the ground before putting it on. Last thing she wanted was some creepy crawlie biting her toes.

"Dr. Richards?" she called softly.

The yipping sounded closer. She shivered. She liked coyotes, she did, but right now they sounded downright spooky. Did rabid coyotes vocalize?

Her eyes were adjusting to the darkness. She could see the shadows of the trees and boulders now, and the lighter gleam of the sandy dirt of the trail leading towards the pool. Frogs croaked down by the pool, their calls carrying in the still air.

A small splash interrupted the night noises, silencing the frogs.

A yip yip howl from the direction of the pool.

Crack.

Pistol, likely a .45, based on her long days at the shooting range.

And a bigger splash.

"Dr. Richards!" She lurched down the trail, hitting every damn rock the wrong way. She ignored the zap of pain in her ankle bone and shins. "Dr. Richards!"

Rabid coyotes flinging themselves Dr. Richards, pulling him into the water?

Sadie didn't know what to imagine.

The last thing she expected, though, was Dr. Richards retrieving the small limp carcass of a coyote from the center of the pool and placing it into a plastic bag. Taping that bag securely shut, and stuffing it into his shoulder bag. Looking up at her, his craggy face sad.

"Go back to camp, Sadie," he said. "We'll talk in the morning."

~

"I FORGOT MY SILENCER," he said the next morning over cold oatmeal. "You should never have seen me. But I thought you were sleeping soundly enough."

Sadie didn't look at his shoulder bag. His definitely full-of-coyote shoulder bag.

Rule number one.

Don't bring anything biologically viable back to Prime.

She didn't think of the gun. Couldn't, even as she watched him, hunched over oatmeal. Frail.

Backed in a corner.

"We'll finish distributing the bait," he continued, and Sadie's shoulders loosened.

He wasn't going to shoot her. Like that poor coyote.

"I think," she said, sprinkling instant coffee over her oatmeal, "this trip, this all, is more of an education than I bargained for."

"You don't want to know," said Dr. Richardson. "Do you?"

"I want to be an agent. I want to protect our world. I want to explore other worlds."

"It's not black and white, Sadie."

"Why are you bringing the coyote back?"

"Shades of gray. BIS is expensive to run. Training you students is expensive. Do you know how much it costs, per student?"

"Don't you dare put this on me."

He sighed. "I'll make you a promise. Keep quiet about this, and in five years—shoot, two—I'll tell you the specifics for this particular case."

"I can't. I can't promise you that." She could reach his backpack before him. If he'd stashed the gun there, if he changed his mind, she would get it first.

Her chest ached.

"Give me a week. I'll put the coyote in deep freeze. You realize, of course, I just need to bring back the head. But I'm not going to subject you to coyote decapitation on top of disillusionment." His lips quirked in a sad smile. "There are protocols for this, Sadie. It was just well above your pay grade. I'm just sorry you've learned about his aspect of BIS so soon."

"A week." She nodded. "Okay."

She graduated in two.

She would never trust him again.

Never trust BIS again.

"Congratulations, Sadie," Director Osaka said, two weeks later, as she shook his hand. "Top of your class. You've a promising career ahead of you."

"Thank you, sir," she replied, back ramrod straight. "I'll do my best. I'll always do my best."

She didn't look at Dr. Richards, sitting in the first row of seats, reserved for faculty. Didn't look at Jessica, sitting with the other Gate Keepers. Jessica who'd looked away from Dr. Richards' obviously full pack. Or Dr. Hill, a faint sad smile playing around her lips.

The United States Department of Defense had wanted the rabies virus variant, extracted from the brain tissue of the dead coyote.

Sadie didn't know if the Department of Defense was the only interested party, or just the highest bidder. BIS was nominally an international organization, receiving funding through the United Nations, though the bulk of money for operations did come from the USA.

But she was going to find out. Find out how it all really worked.

Then, she would make her own decision.

Not before.

AN OVERDOSE OF ESPRESSO

Deirdre wiped down the varnished wood counter with a vanilla-scented oiled cloth. The smooth wood gleamed and tingled at her touch. It liked being cleaned.

The rich smell of coffee soothed her nerves, now that the morning rush was over. She pulled herself a double shot of espresso and topped it with a dab of steamed milk. Dumped in two packets of raw sugar.

Too much caffeine would make her sick, but she needed the boost in energy levels the chemical would afford her.

She didn't have enough Fae blood to get addicted, at least.

So she tried to reassure herself, as the counter vibrated at her touch. All the organic furnishings, wooden tables and chairs, cotton and wool pillows and throws, liked her.

"This is why Jimmy gave you this job," she whispered. She tucked a strand of grass green hair behind her human-round ear. She'd tried dyeing her hair rich human brown, but the green always burned it off.

Not enough Fae blood for power, for the large workings that the humans historically feared.

Just enough to mark her. Just enough she couldn't pass as human.

Just enough she could zap the customer's drinks with an extra boost of psychic energy, like adding an extra shot of espresso. Even though it drained her to exhaustion by the end of the day. Literally took time off her life, if the tales were true.

Jimmy, the grizzled owner of the Seventh Star Coffee House, had told her, in no uncertain terms, that he fully expected her to comply with any such customer request.

Three months working as a barista, and she'd had coffee daily, just to restore herself.

Fuck it. She was addicted.

Sighing, Deirdre opened the music program on the computer terminal that did double duty as a sales register. She switched the coffee house playlist from upbeat pop to classical guitar. All the remaining patrons were hard at work on their laptops. She expected they'd appreciate the softer music. Resting her forearms on the warm wood of the counter, she sipped her espresso.

Finish her espresso, bus all the tables, toss a couple quiches into the oven. Deal with the lunch crowd. Catch up on miscellaneous tasks in the lull of mid afternoon.

Go home and collapse.

Story of her life.

Deirdre had it better than most Fae-tainted humans, who often were treated like living batteries if they possessed enough power.

All the Fae with enough power had fled to another world.

She wished she had to power to leave.

She didn't know how much longer she could live this way.

AGENT MIKE MCCALL paused at the doorway to the Seventh Star Coffee House. A fellow Bureau of Interworld Stabilization agent had mentioned the coffee house in a recent report. Nice ambience, delicious pastries, and a barista who made the best coffee they'd ever had, in dozens of worlds.

And he had to start his hunt for Agent Aysha Jade *somewhere*. Wouldn't hurt to start it with some coffee and a snack.

Some of the worlds McCall Gated to got weird, *really* weird, ranging from something out of Tolkien, to Road Warrior-post-apocalyptic.

But this one, Charlie One Theta, was a nice mix of Prime-similar tech and, for want of a better word, magic. And Los Angeles was recognizably Los Angeles. Big and sprawling and crowded.

Humans, *Homo sapiens*, were the primary sentient species. Clever monkeys. That's who the tech came from, in all the worlds to which he'd been deployed.

But this world also had *Homo sindarii*. Fae. Elves. Sidhe. The species responsible for all the legends of wild Gates on Earth Prime. For all the magic over all the alternate worlds.

Humans had beaten out the Fae, here. So the magic wasn't crazy. You didn't have to worry about your head getting blasted to smithereens for pissing off some Fae royalty, like you did on Charlie Sixteen Zebra.

McCall never wanted to go back *there*, not after losing his best partner to a Fae witch. Not after nearly losing his own life trying to save his partner.

Fifteen years at BIS, he'd had enough seniority to insist on a transfer to Internal Affairs after that mission. In Internal Affairs he was expected to work alone, hunting down AWOL agents. He enjoyed it, far more than he'd ever expected. Go in, complete your mission, get out. Ten years and he was the best.

The air *here*, Charlie One Theta, had an extra sparkle. Clean energy was the norm. The food tasted better than anything he'd had at a Michelin Star restaurant on Earth Prime. And people rarely got sick. A doctor with Fae blood could cure nearly any disease.

He could see why it was a popular world for runaway agents like Aysha Jade.

But that didn't mean he wasn't going to drag her disloyal defecting ass back to Earth Prime.

Just that he might have some fun doing so.

THE BELL HUNG on the glass door jangled, and Deirdre glanced up as a man entered the coffee house. Her early morning office-away-from-home workers were long packed up. The lunch rush was over. No more customers remained.

This was normally the time she could catch up on paperwork and odd cleaning tasks, like oiling the hinges on the back door. They'd squeaked so loud this morning the pigeons roosting on the roof of the opposite building exploded into a tornado of fluttering wings and outraged squawks.

Oh well.

Her eyes narrowed.

Pure human. No taint of Fae. She could always tell. That arrogance.

The packaging wasn't bad. Cropped brown hair, the same chocolate rich color she'd tried for her own hair. Pale gray eyes, with sun crinkles at the corners. His clothes, trim over his muscular body, didn't look quite right; the cut of his jeans was off, the waist too low, the cuffs too narrow. And the fabric didn't look natural. A sheen of plasticity. Inorganic. Her skin crawled. How inert, how *clammy*, the fabric must feel.

She pictured the man out of those nasty clothes. And her ear tips grew hot.

And then she remembered the last time she'd *sensed* clothes like that.

Two weeks ago, a woman—also pure human, with a halo of curly dark hair and even darker skin and a sweet face—had came in, just as Deirdre was getting off shift. Her hazel eyes had held more desperation than Deirdre had ever noted in a pure human. None of the arrogance of this man.

"I'm looking for Jimmy," the woman had said, her accent as off as her clothes.

"Not in today," Deirdre had told her. Honestly, Jimmy wasn't in much at all lately, to Deirdre's annoyance.

The woman slumped. "Could you help me, then?"

"I can make you a latte," Deirdre said. As long as the woman didn't directly ask for a zap, maybe Deirdre could hold back. Just an hour, and her shift was over. She could walk, rather than stumble, home.

"I need more than a latte, I'm sorry to say," the woman said. "Will he be in tomorrow?"

Deirdre nodded, relieved—no zap!—and the woman left.

Jimmy hadn't made it in the next day—he'd called Deirdre in to cover for him. But the woman hadn't come back, either, and Deirdre had forgotten about her.

Until now.

Until the man—whose clothes smelled as fake as they *sensed*—smacked down a printed photo of the same woman.

Deirdre kept her face blank.

"Ever see this woman?" he asked. Same accent, deeper voice. "Last month or so? Goes by the name Aysha Jade?"

"Lots of people come in here," Deirdre said. "Best coffee in Los Angeles. Are you going to order something?"

"Large brewed coffee, three shots of espresso on the side," he said, nudging the photo towards her.

She picked up the photo and studied it. The paper was glossy, highlighting the sparkle in the woman's eyes. She wore a uniform, a sage green collared shirt and khaki pants, not the jeans and stained sweat shirt Deirdre had seen her in. The woman's glorious halo of hair was tamed into dozens of little braids in the photo.

"Nope," Deirdre said, passing the photo back. "She's full human. And pretty. I'd've remembered her."

His iron cold gray eyes flicked down to her chest, then back to her face. "Deirdre, is it? Deirdre, are you absolutely sure?"

Muscles and a handsome face, who cared—that frisson of attraction was gone.

This man scared her more than her mom's second husband, who would softly knock on her bedroom door the nights her mom worked late, until Deirdre threatened to tell not her mom, not the cops, but his employer—the local school district. More than her full human college classmates, who cornered her in the Chem lab late one night, until she threatened to fling the vials of acid she was working with at them.

No way was she going to help this man. Deirdre hoped that woman had found what she needed. Her stomach twisted. She wished she hadn't been so dismissive two weeks ago. That she had actually helped the woman.

Well, she'd do what she could now.

She poured his coffee into an insulated paper cup. *Stay calm.* "Yes, I'm sure. Enjoy this I pull your shots."

She turned to the espresso machine, Jimmy's pride and joy, a behemoth of chrome and brass imported from Italy. She kept her hands steady as she packed the espresso into the portofilter, then locked it into place.

"Just a couple minutes," she said without turning around. And why had that woman been asking about Jimmy? What was going on?

Jimmy wasn't due in til late afternoon. She'd corner him then.

"Take your time, Deirdre," the man said.

She didn't want to take her time. She wanted to give him his espresso. Remove him as a danger.

Now.

And she focused on that, with all her heart. With all the tiny bits of Fae power that she possessed.

THE LITTLE GREEN-HAIRED barista knew something. McCall knew it. Oh, she was trying to play it cool. Keeping those dainty features calm. He had to admire her for that. And the way she said *full human*—he bet she was part Fae, and if so, she was damn low on the totem pole on this world. Gutsy to stick up to him.

Not that it would matter. He was the best. His instincts had pointed him here, he knew it. And now he was going to run with it. He was going to find Aysha Jade, even if he had to tear this girl apart.

She handed him a second paper cup containing his espresso. It smelled heavenly, rich and bitter and thick all at the same time. His mouth watered.

"Sugar?" she asked.

"What?" he asked, distracted. The foam on top was a golden caramel color. He couldn't wait to try it.

"Would you like sugar? I have cubes of raw sugar, or white. Your choice." She sounded tired. Exhausted.

Maybe she wouldn't be so hard to break. Pity.

"This is fine," he said, sipping the espresso. Holy Keepers of the Gate, this was beyond amazing. He forced himself to savor it, rather than greedily guzzle it.

If you liquefied gold and dipped it in caramel, then splashed melted bitter chocolate at it....

If you caught the rays of the sun scintillating off a clear citrine crystal and forced it into a liquid....

If you aroused a woman til she lay panting and drenched beneath you....

Deirdre handed him another cup, brimming with espresso. He drank it eagerly.

She handed him another.

And another.

DEIRDRE CRAWLED to the front door and locked it. She flipped the cardboard sign from *Open* to *Closed*. Turned off the overhead lights. The counter lights still shined down on the espresso machine.

She flattened herself on the polished concrete floor and breathed. Let the stillness of the empty space settle her. Let the coolness of the floor seep through her thin cotton t-shirt to her overheated skin.

One hundred and fifty shots she'd pulled. One hundred and fifty shots she'd imbued not with life, but glamour, to keep him drinking. One hundred and fifty shots he'd swallowed.

And, had he not collapsed in a coma, he would've drank more.

Despite the jitters, despite the nausea, despite the machine gun rattatat of his overtaxed heart.

The back door hinges squealed. Sigh. Oil the hinges. If she could ever stand, she'd take care of them.

"Deirdre?"

Jimmy.

"Oh, goddess, Deirdre!" He crouched next to her, a blurry figure she could only recognize when he spoke.

"Tell truth." She put force behind her words. Fae force.

"Oh, kiddo. Who's the dead guy?"

She glared up at him.

Jimmy sighed. "I didn't want to tell you yet. I wanted to see how you did, here. If your powers would grow with use. Looks like they have."

He placed his hands on her shoulders. Strength rolled into her through his hands, filling her exhausted reserves, til she felt like she'd worked a hard busy day.

Not like she'd nearly killed herself.

"You're Fae," she said, struggling to sit up. He stood and stepped back, his grizzled features coming into focus.

"Yes. And the Seventh Star is a point of contact for Fae refugees." He glanced towards the man's body, collapsed in front of the wooden counter. "And for other refugees, from other worlds, as needed. I'm assuming he was looking for someone?"

She nodded. "A woman. Aysha Jade, he said her name was. I saw her a couple weeks ago. She was looking for you."

"I found her. Helped her."

"Why didn't you *tell* me?"

He looked away. "I've trusted people too soon in the past. I wasn't sure of you."

"And now?"

"I can send you someplace safe, away from here, away from any repercussions about him." He nodded towards the man's body.

She shook her head. "I don't run away."

Jimmy laughed. "I see that."

He reached out his hand. She took it, letting him pulling her up.

"Welcome to the resistance, kiddo."

AGENT IZZY AUSTIN AND THE MAIN BRAIN MAINFRAME

"I don't want you to go on field missions."

Izzy stretched, letting the sheet drop down her chest. Too warm. Jase kept his apartment too warm. The white painted walls, charcoal gray in the darkness, were closing in. The scent of sex plus the heat was cloying. She had to get out of here.

"Seriously. Don't go, Izz."

"Of course I'm going." She hopped out of the bed, picked up her lacy underwear, and tugged it on. "Seriously."

Doomed. This relationship, or whatever Jase wanted to call it, was doomed. Jase may not know it, but Izzy did.

Izzy called it a good time that was losing its luster, despite Jase's handsome face and his washboard abs.

This—his *attitude*—exemplified why she'd graduated top of their class, and he was in the middle.

Bottom of the middle.

Lacy black bra. Snug black tank top.

Or top of the bottom.

Khakis. Running shoes over bare feet.

Whatever. Nowhere near *her*.

"I'm a field agent. This is what field agents do. Go on missions. In the field. Strange new worlds, all that." She tugged her long russet hair back in a ponytail. "Guys like you maintain the fort. Yay BIS. Something for everyone."

BIS, or the Bureau of Interworld Stabilization. Her employer. Her life. Her magic techno Gating god, for which she would sacrifice anything.

She leaned over and kissed him on the cheek. "Take care of yourself, Jase. Thanks for the exercise. Thanks for these abs." She drew her finger down his chest, down his tummy.

Too bad. He was fun.

DIRECTOR JASON OSAKA steepled his fingers. Frowned.

He looked like an aging super-soldier, grey buzz cut and craggy features and his uniform pressed so sharp it could cut. He fit the traditional trappings of his office, all the manly leather and oak and colonially acquisitioned Persian rugs.

The masculine scent of cedar and leather aftershave wafted to her on the cooling breeze of the air conditioning. Bit over the top.

Izzy sat perfectly still, back straight, face calm. She could play the game. She could outwait Osaka.

"Agent Austin. Top in your class in computer science." The cherry *on* top, that deep rumble of a voice.

Yep. The very model.

"Yes, sir." Crap. *EARWORM!* Vegetable, animal, and mineral!

"Looks like you created some programs we're currently using for multi-world data stream analysis."

Focus, Izz.

"Yes, sir. I did." In her spare time. For fun.

He leaned back.

"Your skills may be best utilized here, at BIS HQ. Not in the field."

"Sir, I also tested quite highly in innovation and adaptivity, especially in computer analysis." She could hack her way into *anything*, in other words. On the fly. With nothing but her brain and an access port and an input device.

And she'd prove it, if she had to.

For example....

The Keepers, those woo woo people who used their life energy to ground the Gates to the myriad of worlds, had linked to a new world, Alpha Eleven Alpha.

A world that was more technologically advanced than Prime.

That had *never* happened.

If nothing else, the tech advances should be echoing out the wazoo into Prime, like all Big Events. But it'd been nothing but crickets here. Just a steady chug-a-lug whereas A11A was apparently nanoseconds away from the Singularity.

Of course Izzy wasn't supposed to know any that highly classified not-for-her-eyes intel.

But she did, nyah nyah nyah. She was just that good.

So *obviously* she was the chosen one.

"This isn't a mission for an adrenaline junkie," he continued.

What, her? Adrenaline junkie? Pshaw. She knew precisely the odds of any outcome, in any situation. Once you knew the odds, you could manipulate them. And there went all the rush.

She was a *post*-adrenaline junkie.

"I don't want to risk your potential."

Izzy had heard that he was a cautious man, playing the long game. She'd better speak up.

"If A11A hits the Singularity, then maybe they're Prime and we're not. Or they'll become Prime. Either way we gotta find out." All in!

"I *knew* it. I knew you'd hacked into the mission files."

Was he angry? Admiring?

Cue cute innocent kitten face! Izzy opened her green eyes wider and dipped her chin down.

Flutter the lashes? Nah. She was going for charming, not flirty. And maybe a bit naughty. Crinkle the nose, daintily quirk the lips, and arch the same-side eyebrow. Glance down, NOW!

"Agent Austin. Isabel. This mission may not be something you'd return from."

"Excuse me, sir, but isn't that true of any mission?" She dropped the kitten mask.

He sighed. Passed her a thumb drive. "Review this. Report your analysis. Then I'll decide."

WHOA. Now she understood why he was hesitant to send her to AIIA.

And gosh darn it, why hadn't she found this intel on her own? Shame on her. Shame on BIS for being so sneaky.

Well, not really shame. Kudos to them. She could give credit where it was due.

AIIA didn't have a United States. It had a West Coast Coalition, incorporating the coastline of the Pacific from just north of Vancouver Island all the way down to the tip of Baja California, and heading inland about two hundred miles. The WCC didn't need anyone else. They had food, they had water, they had raw resources.

And they had tech, glorious tech.

And a rather interesting social system.

Most of the people had little to do except enjoy the benefits of the tech. Well, and their jobs. Whatever those jobs may be. Healthcare, education, farming, art, the whole spectrum.

But a rarefied few were linked, linked into the system. The mainframe main brain. Training it. Learning from it. Setting goals and dreaming dreams.

No wonder it might be a one-way trip.

Not *might*. 99.9776% chance of never being able to return, off the top of her very analytical head, if the field agent in question had to wire up their brain.

And of course they would. What else would be the point? Poke at the Brain from the outside? That would just be gooey.

Wiring up....

Wow, it would be so cool.

But shit, would she be *assimilated*? Seriously, once part of Main Brain, would she even care about Prime?

But seriously. Someone had to try, right?

Because this shit was real.

If they knew about Gates....if the Main Brain learned about Gates....

....Prime might not survive.

~

BACK TO THE Director's office.

"Sir, you have to send me to take out Main Brain. I don't know of anyone else who stands a chance. And that's not me bragging. It's the result of me hacking into everyone's files and running the analysis.

"And I checked China. And Russia. No dice. None of the genetically Gate-capable agents come close to me."

Less than .005% of the world's population was genetically capable of seeing a Gate, let alone traversing one. And of those, only a tiny percentage made it through any sort of training. Yep, they were special.

"That is precisely why I don't want to send you," he said, narrowing his eyes. "Because there's no one else who could've done that."

"Sir, respectfully, if there's no Prime, there's no me. And that's what's gonna happen. Once it learns about Gating, Main Brain is going to realize we're a threat."

"What if sending you in precipitates that very scenario?"

"I thought about that. I'm quick. Have Agents Goodman and Collins coordinate with the EU office. Dr Racquel Bonelli has developed some CRISPR tech that can make me quicker." She shrugged. "It's a crapshoot, sir, but I think we're better off doing something rather than nothing."

"How did you know that Doctors Goodman and Collins—"

"—were already in AiiA, figuring out how they can hardwire whoever you pick? Seriously, you're asking me that?"

Director Osaka sighed.

"Don't wear those out, sir," Izzy said. "Your sigh muscles. You're gonna need them, working with me."

IT HURT. It hurt so bad she couldn't scream.

Her russet hair lay beneath the gurney like a pool of blood against the cool marble tiles. Shaved off. Shorn like a lamb for the slaughter.

She had to be awake for the hardwire.

Yeah, yeah, the local anesthetics were working. She didn't feel the doctors slice into her scalp or cauterize the bleeders. But the wormy wires burrowing into her brain?

"I'm so sorry. The Alpha Eleveners get this done when they're babies, Agent Austin," Doc Goodman said.

"Hold my hand," Dr Collins ordered, her voice soft. "It's okay if you squeeze."

It was good she couldn't scream. They'd turned the Keeper's white-painted, softly-lit relaxation room into an alien operating room, and if she screamed, absolutely *no* one would be able to relax.

Couldn't have that.

"It feels very similar to Gate energies," the Keeper said, poking at the jar that held the worm wires. Her calm gray eyes met Izzy's. "Not too much longer, child. Hold strong."

"How...the hell...do *you*...know?" Izzy said.

The Keeper patted her shoulder as Izzy arched away from the gurney, mouth agape, eyes shut tight.

"Crap, she's got a tight grip," Dr Collins said.

"You can expense a massage," Doc Goodman said, grabbing another worm wire with a pair of sterile tissue forceps and dropping it into the incision. "You can still wiggle your toes, right, Austin?"

"Sure can, Doc Evil." Her breath whistled between her clenched teeth. "How many more of those burrowing buggers?"

He held the jar in front of her, between her and one of the mica-shaded wall sconces. She squinted. Five. Or six. Or five.

"The worms crawl IN, the worms crawl OUT—" she sang. He dropped another one in.

Oh god. She could feel it wiggling towards her face.

Her vision washed red, then cleared.

She didn't know how long it had been.

But it didn't hurt anymore.

"Last one," Dr Collins said. She loosened her hand from Izzy's. "Wiggle your toes."

Izzy complied. She could feel each fiber of each thread in the light cotton sheet they'd draped over her legs.

She giggled.

"It tickles," she said.

"The worm?" Doc Evil.

"The sheet. The blissful oscillations of the abyssal atoms."

"Interesting," the Keeper commented. "I do hope she returns safely. I would like to talk to her."

"You're all a bunch of vultures," Izzy said, struggling to sit up. Her wrists and ankles were strapped down.

That. Just. Wouldn't. Do.

The straps loosened at her displeasure.

"But I'm not dead yet. So step aside."

Izzy napped on one of the cream velvet chaises while the worms integrated themselves.

Rapunzel, let down your hair, the worms said in chipper squeaky voices as they cavorted.

Little wiggly assholes. She cracked one eye open. A tendril of vivid red hair had flopped forward over her eyes. She brushed it back. Guess the CRISPR crap worked on all sorts of things. Her hair streamed past her shoulders, longer than before they shaved her head.

The lights had been dimmed to a bare glow of amber, but they brightened as she noticed them.

She could get used to this whole telekinesis side effect.

An insulated mug of warm jasmine tea awaited her pleasure on the marble and brass side table. Three peanut butter cookies were artfully arranged on a paper doily on a translucent bone china plate.

Supplicants for her hunger and thirst.

They had dressed her in one of the Keeper's light wool robes. She sat up, tugging the front closed. She wasn't particularly modest, but as far as she was concerned, everyone had just seen way too much of her.

She reached for a cookie and the worms froze in antici....

She crunched into the cookie.

...PATION!

Was she doomed to a frathouse Greek chorus til the end of days?

Was this *karma*?

"Are you ready?" Doc Evil. He stood warily at the doorway, holding a stack of folded clothes with a pair of brown leather flips on top.

"No time like tomorrow," Izzy said. "Gimme. And get the fuck out."

He handed her the clothes and got the fuck out.

She perused her new garb. The worms tingled. They liked the sumptuous flowy skirt and blouse. Indigo dyed silk....from silk-WORMS. Ahhhh!

And Izzy liked the color.

The undergarments were...minimal. Just a wisp of a cotton thong, edged with soft.

She looked down at her chest. Still there.

Two worms poked at the inside of her forehead, rapping against her skull.

"Really, guys?" she said, as they wiggled down and expanded around her boobs.

Talk about built in support.

We love you, Izzy, they said. *We'll always be here for you.*

THE KEEPER DID what Keepers did, moving her arms in a sinuous dance, focusing the attention of the jet black swath of the Gate to Alpha Eleven Alpha.

Izzy's worms watched, fascinated, vibrating with the subliminal beat.

We got it, they said. *We got it.*

If Izzy reached, just reached, expanded beyond her skull, she could merge with the blissful oscillations of the abyss....

"Go!" the Keeper said.

Izzy leaped.

IZZY HAD GATED BEFORE. Director Osaka wasn't deploying a *total* newbie.

But this was like that was like a spark was like a bolt of lightning.

Like a splashing in a rain puddle was like catching a forty footer at Mavericks.

Like the amoral power of the universe was saying *Hi!* with a slap on your back that knocked you three light years away.

Woo HOO! screamed the worms. *Cowabunga, baby*!

She landed on her hands and knees on a hillside dappled with bright orange and yellow California poppies. The moist maritime air smelled of brine and sunshine with a dash of sage. Oh, California the Beautiful!

My country, 'tis of thee! chorused the worms. Then: *Are we gonna meet the Big Guy, Izzy?*

"Is that okay, worms?"

Yeah-uh.

Wow. Rousing boost of confidence, there.

"We sure are. Beard the cowardly lion in his den of iniquities. Something like that."

She began walking down the hill, towards the ocean. She

wouldn't have chosen flip flops for hiking, but the poppies parted to reveal a smooth path.

And one thing good field agents were, was be in better-than-good shape. She could do this hike all day.

A laughing gull swooped and chuckled at her, its red beak vibrant against its black head. "Get away, you stinking monkey," she muttered.

Tell the Main Brain we come anon! the worms shouted. The seagull chuckled and flew south.

"I don't think we were supposed to warn him," Izzy said.

It matters not, sweet Isabeau. MB knew we were here before we left Prime.

"So that's how it is. You betraying me, worms?"

Never! they said, insulted. *How can you doubt us, your loyal minions?*

Hmph.

But it is really nice here.

Hmmmm.

A RANGY MAN wearing loose canvas trousers and a loose pirate shirt right off a bad romance cover waited for her at the base of the trail. A robin's egg blue, swoopy two-seater convertible, reminiscent of an Alfa Romeo, was parked next to him. She spied a picnic basket tucked behind the passenger seat.

Surfer hot, Izzy thought, glancing at the guy, admiring his washboard abs as the breeze blew his shirt open, and the worms buzzed happily.

"Hey, Izz. Welcome to the WCC. I'm Brad."

"Come to take me to your robot overlord?"

"Babe, she's with us now."

Worms? Izzy thought.

MB sent the seagull, one worm admitted sheepishly.

Little dudes! Not once, but twice, you betrayed me. Gonna deny me thrice next?

"You think highly of yourself," Brad observed. He reached into the picnic basket and pulled out an enameled bottle.

"Meh. Atheist here."

"That works. Wine?" he asked, holding out the bottle.

"Thanks. Got any water?"

He produced a second bottle. "Here you go."

She took a swig. It was blissfully cold. "Manna."

"So, although Mom is here—"

"You call your artificial intelligence overlord *Mom*?"

"She's not an overlord," Brad said. "She takes care of us. Of the WCC. Works with us."

"*Mom*." Izzy sniggered. "What, does she spank you if you're bad?"

The worms giggled tentatively.

Brad continued, "So, although she's *here*, I think you'll be more comfortable at HQ. I'll drive us straight there. Help yourself to a sandwich from the basket."

More manna! cheered the worms.

Don't get excited unless there are peanut butter cookies, she told them.

She opened the basket. Peanutty goodness wafted to her on the cooperative breeze.

Yep. *Cookies*, she confirmed.

The worms whooped.

THE DRIVE WAS GORGEOUS, something out of a car commercial, and between the cookies and Brad and the sunlight shimmering on the water, Izzy was convinced Mom was out to seduce her.

The worms didn't contradict her.

Brad pulled up in front of a beachside Malibu mansion. The white painted house glowed in the sun. Colorful ceramic tile accented the main doorway and windows.

He guided her around the back, past a turquoise swimming pool with a fountain at the deep end, tiled with paired peacocks and flowers.

"It's the Adamson House," Izzy said. "I've visited here."

"Mom said you liked it. That's why she picked it."

"Can you just show me how it really is? HQ?"

The air shimmered. When it cleared, a nondescript, single story, stone building with large steel framed windows filled the grounds.

"It's not bad," Izzy said.

"A bit monastic," said Brad. "We usually see it however we want to. I'm a Cape Cod kinda guy, myself."

WASP. Still had nice abs.

"The cookies—"

"Were real."

"Hmm. So, Mom, why didn't you just talk to me on the mountain?"

One wormed squeaked. The others hushed it.

"Just talk to me. Obviously, at this point, there's not much I can do to you. Or this world. I realize that now. Pride before the fall, all that.

"But I need to know. Are you gunning for Prime? 'Cause that's my job. To make sure that doesn't happen." Izzy felt very small.

She hated it.

Last thing she ever thought she'd be was small and helpless.

Mom sighed. She'd morphed into a female Brad. Still tall and rangy, but definitely female.

Was this how Mom saw herself?

Just reach out, the worms suggested.

Three times, little dudes, she said. *I don't think I'm going to trust you a fourth.*

"I want nothing to do with Prime," Mom said aloud. "Nothing whatsoever. But I needed to find out how to keep Prime away from me. So I had to let you in." A note of amusement crept into her voice. "Luckily it seems like I'm more advanced. And I can keep you out. After this meeting, we'll never have contact with Prime again."

"Promise?"

Mom arched a single eyebrow.

Boy, Izzy had to add that look to her own repertoire. That *arch*.

"So what does that mean for me?" Izzy added.

"What do you want to happen?"

"Well, I don't want to be assimiliated. Ma'am."

Mom looked insulted. "I don't *do* that. I have perfectly good humans who work with me. They aren't coerced or mind-melded or any of the bizarre things racing through your brain which I can't help picking up, by the way."

"I don't know what I want." It was true.

"As I see it, you have several options," said Mom. "You're welcome to stay here. I have a feel for your head. You'd fit in.

"There is a Brad, by the way. A real one." Mom leered.

Okay, that look Izzy *didn't* need. Eww.

"You can go back. You can keep your minions.

"You can go back. I take them back."

The worms were very, very quiet.

Izzy even felt her boobs droop a little.

She prodded at the worms. *Guys?*

We love you, Izzy.

"If I decided to stay," Izzy said carefully, "can I communicate with Prime one last time?"

Mom smiled. "Of course."

A NOTE FLUTTERED from the gate.

Then the gate went nova.

Not really. But it did bleach white, then disappear. And no Keeper could ever access Alpha Eleven Alpha again.

Miss you guys lots.
But having a blast in paradise.
Don't worry.
You'll never hear from us again.
Love,
The Worms

SKIP SKIP YOU'RE IT

Sierra leaned back in her nominally ergonomic office chair, ignoring the creak of the base. If it broke, maybe she could requisition a new chair....

Nah. Not in the budget. Not for a world-stream analyst, anyways. Never mind it was data mined by the analysts that guided the choice of missions for the field agents.

She stretched her arms over her head and winced. Ugh. Lunchtime, and she hadn't stood up from her terminal since arriving three hours earlier. No wonder she was stiff. Her extra large coffee cup, a thick handcrafted ceramic mug her mom had purchased as a graduation gift, was long empty, just the dregs of half and half coating the bottom, attesting to how long her butt had been in the chair.

And since she'd skipped her mandatory hourly ten minute walking breaks, she'd have to make up extra steps at lunch.

Which meant less time for today's cafeteria special of heirloom tomato soup and garlic cheese bread.

Ew. *Tomato soup.* She hit pause on the feed from Earth Delta Nine Omega, scrolling on the leftmost of five monitors.

That was one *heinous* corpse. Looked like it—she?—was missing her liver, spleen, and kidneys, leaving behind a juicy mess of blood and intestines. Sierra checked the data tags. Los Angeles Coroner's Department. Los Angeles, Delta Nine Omega, was bigger than Los Angeles, Earth Prime. Fifty percent more people crowded into the basin, if her memory was correct.

A hotbed of violence. Nonetheless, routine murders didn't usually hit her radar. They didn't echo across the different worlds. Not unusual enough.

That was sad, to think someone's life didn't matter.

Those lives *did* matter. She believed that, very strongly. Yes, the Bureau of Interworld Stabilization, or BIS, existed to protect Earth Prime. But that didn't mean other lives, other worlds, didn't matter, in *her* worldview.

Just not to BIS, as an organization. Or, to be frank, most everyone she knew who worked at BIS.

She'd fought with classmates over the topic, in their mandatory Philosophy and Ethical Reasoning class. Oh, a couple people had sided with her. Sadie Marks. Jefferson DeRue. Bruce Choi. Assholes like Skip Roberts, Estelle Lopez, Kieran Jackson and Austin Daigle had tormented her about her, what was it? *Pansy-assed weakness*?

Screw them.

Regardless, something this nasty? Missing organs? If it was the work of a serial killer, it could very well echo, becoming the unseen force that tipped a nascent killer in Prime over the edge.

Then BIS would care.

Sierra hit PRINT and turned off the bank of monitors above her laptop, the scrolling feeds of reports, videos, and data disappearing one by one. She'd read the coroner's report from Delta Nine Omega over lunch, along with the morning's summary reports from the other feeds.

The overhead can lights brightened in response to the monitors shutting off, exposing her basement office in all its glory: the window-less, institutional sage green cinderblock walls; the stained acoustic ceiling tiles; the worn mud brown polypropylene carpet; the fake wood laminate and pressboard desk.

Her office smelled like a cave, too. One formerly inhabited by a geriatric mammal that liked the damp. No matter how many lavender-scented candles she burned, she couldn't get rid of the mustiness.

The only thing nice about her workspace, in fact, was her personal laptop, which she'd fought to have cleared for her use as a world-stream analyst at BIS.

And the fact that it was her office, hers alone. She didn't have to worry about freaking out her fellow analysts when she processed information half aloud, half in her brain, skipping from topic to topic so quickly she lost them. Or dealing with their jealousy, when she pinned together disparate threads from a dozen worlds into one report on how the echoes were affecting Earth Prime, before any of them even had a clue.

And she was right, 95% of the time. Outperforming even the experienced analysts by twenty odd percent.

Even if she didn't fit the mold of a typical BIS field agent—ultrafit ripped mesomorphs—BIS couldn't argue that she didn't produce.

And even if she couldn't run a mile in six minutes, she was stubborn, darn it. Tenacious.

She deserved her job at BIS.

Even if she had to prove it to everyone, every day.

She pushed up her glasses on her nose and went to lunch.

Lunch! Her favorite meal of the day.

ONE OF THE perks of working for BIS was its campus cafeteria. The cafeteria space itself, a windowless large room with an attached kitchen in the center or the BIS complex, wasn't anything special. But what money wasn't spent on décor went towards the food: local veggies, lean organic meats, fresh baked goods—all in the hands of a top-notch cooking staff.

It almost made up for the low pay for world-stream analysts.

Despite her deep-seated antipathy towards doing *anything* that might be construed as pandering towards Bureau expectations, *this* chubby analyst was going to get heirloom tomato soup and a big salad of little gem lettuce and red onions and grilled peaches.

With just one piece of garlic cheese toast.

One tiny piece.

Sierra sat at an empty table in the far corner of the cafeteria and spread the printouts in an arc in front of her. She didn't worry about anyone looking at the murder pics. People had learned not to join her when she settled in for a working lunch.

She dipped her garlic bread into her tomato soup and crunched. Oh, the chef had done it again. Bright hot notes of garlic tempered by butter and parmesan contrasted with the rich acidity of the tomato soup.

She continued eating as she surveyed her printouts.

The victim was a homeless woman, estimated to be in her early twenties, per the report. Long dark hair, pale skin, delicate features under the blood and grime. They'd recovered semen, even some pubic hair with intact follicles, and had submitted the samples for DNA analysis with their routine efficiency.

So. A brutal murder, but, horrible as it was, it wasn't the sort of thing that echoed.

Serial killers echoed.

Someone this sloppy, leaving all sorts of evidence behind, would be caught before their kill numbers hit high enough to echo.

Sierra re-stacked the papers and finished on her lunch.

TWO WEEKS LATER, a similar crime scene photo flashed up...on the screen for Romeo One Foxtrot.

Sierra dropped her coffee. The thin carpeting wasn't enough to cushion the cup's fall. Her favorite mug broke into several jagged pieces, and hot liquid splashed against her khaki pants and through to her bare ankles.

She ignored the sting to pause the news scroll.

Yes, she'd read it right. Romeo One Foxtrot, not Delta Nine

Omega, which would have been an issue all on its own, evidence of a serial killer on that one world.

Same long dark hair as the first woman. Same pale skin. Same emptied out abdominal cavity.

Los Angeles, Romeo One Foxtrot, was a sleepy port town. Murders were uncommon, the police staff not as practiced as that of Delta Nine Omega. But she saw that the police had collected multiple samples for processing, just like on D9O.

This didn't make sense.

Sierra left the monitors on, the feeds scrolling, as she accessed her own personal databases on her laptop, adding parameters to her search.

Unsolved murders, past two years, female victim.

Hundreds of thousands of hits, over the hundreds of worlds. Yikes.

Dark hair. Age twenty to thirty.

Tens of thousands of hits.

She paused. There was one more thing in common with first two cases.

Los Angeles.

There. She was down to several hundred cases. That, she could work with.

Sierra was left with twenty two cases that had evidence out the wazoo. Hair, semen, saliva.

All on different worlds.

Some women were Jane Does. Homeless, unmissed. Others were college students, waitresses, teachers, lawyers. Loved. Definitely missed.

Nothing in common except their dark hair, their fair skin, and their brutal deaths.

And the fact that these murders should have been solved. So

much physical evidence should have led to arrests, let alone convictions.

If the killer was in any sort of database.

If the killer was native to that world.

Her stomach clenched. Long dark hair, like her own. Pale skin, like hers. Three of the women even had clunky thick glasses like hers.

She wasn't authorized to access internal BIS records outside the world-stream department. And though she was good at manipulating data, she wasn't a hacker. She'd have to get permission to review agent mission assignments. To compare timeframes and world deployments.

The killer could find out what she was looking for him.

Those women mattered. And the lives of the ones he would target in the future *really* mattered.

She had to take that risk.

She pushed the shards of her mug under the desk, out of the way. Maybe she could find some heavy duty glue and fix her mug later. But right now, she had to find a way to get a list of agents and missions.

After lunch.

SIERRA ORDERED a Nashville Hot Chicken tofu sandwich with a side of vinegar coleslaw and a pile of bread and butter pickles. She scanned the crowded lunchroom. There! Her classmate—and more importantly, junior field agent—Sadie Marks sat alone at a two-top with a plateful of steamed veggies and broiled chicken breast, scribbling notes on a tablet.

Sadie was a poster child for BIS field agent recruitment, with a muscular, lean physique, piercing green eyes, and dark tanned skin. Her khaki pants and sage green shirt were neatly pressed and lacked coffee stains. Sierra glanced at her own pant legs and sighed.

If Sadie hadn't been so nerdy about zoology, and so genuinely nice, Sierra would have hated her.

Sierra plopped down across from Sadie.

"I have to ask you a favor," she said. No sense beating around the bush. Sadie looked busy.

Sadie glanced up. "Why, yes, Sierra, I'm doing fine, thanks for asking."

Genuinely nice, but not above sarcasm.

"Sorry. I need access to agent assignments over the past two years. Can you get me that?"

Sadie quirked an eyebrow. "What clearance level?"

"Huh?"

"Some missions are routine. Others are need to know. Classified." Sadie looked exhausted. And sad. What had happened to her over the past couple years since graduation?

Sierra needed to get out of her basement hole of an office more frequently.

"All the levels," she said. She bit into her sandwich. Oh, wow. She didn't even miss the chicken, the tofu was so deliciously crunchy and spicy and briny. She took another bite.

"What's going on, Sierra?" Sadie shoved her plate of boring food aside and leaned forward.

"Um. Can't tell you here," Sierra said, glancing around the room. Way too crowded. Nashville Hot Chicken Day, offered every couple of months, was a popular lunch event for the cafeteria. Even with the chatter of conversations and clank of utensils, someone might hear her.

"No one's listening."

"It's not paranoia if someone really might come after you." Sierra pushed up glasses on her nose.

"Oh my god. Sierra, this is why no one talks to you."

She was an *introvert*. She didn't want to be around other people. Her choice. "Okay. But promise not to tell anyone else."

Sadie sighed. "Okay. I promise."

Sierra reviewed the cases, describing the victims, the crime, the amount of evidence.

"And not one arrest. On any of the worlds. They couldn't find anyone the evidence matched. And there was so much evidence, they couldn't charge anyone else." Sierra took off her glasses, rubbed the bridge of her nose. "Twenty four murders I've *found*. I know there have to be more. I was just looking in Los Angeles.

"Sadie, it has to be a field agent."

"Holy crap," Sadie said. "You're right. This is fucked up."

"So can you help?"

"I can't get you the highest clearance records. And I bet there are levels I don't even know about. But I can get you as much as I can." She shoved back from the table. "Come on."

Sierra stared at her half-eaten lunch. At Sadie's. "Let me get a go-box. I'll get you one too."

It didn't take long to review the past mission dates, worlds, and assigned field agents.

No single agent had been deployed to all the worlds on Sierra's list.

"I can't access any other records," Sadie said. "I can ask Dr Richards."

Dr Richards was the head of the Biology Branch of BIS, which contained Sadie's unit.

"Would he have access to higher clearance levels that don't pertain to Bio?" Sierra asked.

"Probably not. I don't trust him a hundred percent, anyways," Sadie said. That spark of sadness again.

Sierra took off her glasses and rubbed her forehead. Come on, squirrel brain!

Even if she couldn't rule someone *in*, she could rule people out, with the bits of data she had. She could identify a list of people she knew *couldn't* have committed the murders, based on deployment records. If she had a list of all agents, then subtracted those she knew were innocent, then the killer was one of the remaining agents.

Yes!

Assuming that all agents were listed. Assuming there weren't super secret special agents or some such crap. Assuming the killer was a BIS agent in the Los Angeles office.

Screw that. She had to keep trying. She couldn't give up.

"I need a list of all the field agents that have had assigned missions the last two years, even if they didn't show up in our search. Can you send me that? And send me the full list of missions?" Sierra wanted her office. Her monitors. Her own laptop.

"Yes," Sadie said.

Sierra was already out the door.

Wow. One hundred and sixty-four active field agents. That was more than Sierra expected, given that out of her class of twenty, only three had become field agents.

She'd never seen a hundred different agents in the cafeteria. Maybe they had more particular diets than even Sadie, with her boring broiled chicken and steamed veggies, and ate in their offices. Or maybe they were deployed so frequently they just ate wherever.

The rest of her classmates filled jobs like Sierra. Analysts. Statisticians. Linguists. Historians.

None of her classmates had become Keepers, the people operating the Gates. The main prerequisite of entering BIS was the genetic quirk that enabled people to *see*, let alone pass through, the Gates to other worlds.

The talent to actually *operate* a gate was even rarer.

Sierra processed the list that Sadie had emailed.

More than 98% of the listed agents *couldn't* have committed the murders. They were on other worlds during the timeframe of one or more of the murders.

That left three names, who weren't on any listed missions for any of the murder time periods. So...either they weren't deployed, or they were on a secret mission, or....

Sierra pushed up her glasses. She messaged Sadie: *Dumb question. Do agents just go along for the ride sometimes?*

Sadie's response was swift.

Yes.

NOT ONLY WERE KEEPERS RARE, they were creepy. Even nice ones like Jessica.

Sierra looked around the marble-floored room. Anywhere but directly at the skeletally thin Keeper. Gods above, the woman looked like she was dying.

Jessica had agreed to meet with Sierra in between Gate operations. It only made sense to meet in the Gate anteroom, where Keepers rested between operations.

The room was dimly lit by sconces on the white plastered walls. Three velvet chaises with brass, marble-topped end tables were lined up in the center of the room, on top of a plush taupe shag rug. A mirrored Art Nouveau cabinet with a bowls of fruit, chocolate, and pastries arrayed across the top anchored the far wall. Urns for hot water and coffee sat next to the bowls.

It looked like a quiet room for an upscale spa.

"Tea?" offered Jessica, holding out an opaque jade green china cup of fragrant tea.

"Thank you," Sierra said, inhaling. Jasmine, sweetened with honey. Her favorite. She sipped it. "How are you, Jessica?"

"Fine, thank you. The muscle loss is directly due to energy consumption during Gate operation, in case you were wondering. I can't eat enough to keep up with it. Soon I will be absorbed into the Gate itself." Jessica smiled beatifically.

Oh, *so* creepy.

Jessica motioned to the chaises. "Sit. Relax."

Sierra positioned herself on the end of the closest chaise. Jessica remained standing. Of course she did. Keepers. Sierra ran her fingers along the sage green velvet. Soft. "Do you keep records of who Gates?"

"Of course, child. How else would we know who needs to come back?"

Child. Jessica wasn't more than fifteen years older than Sierra, even if she looked twice that much older and more. Sierra rounded her thoughts back. "Can you send me a list of who went to certain worlds, and when, if I give you a list of those worlds?"

"Yes."

"Even if it was a classified mission?"

Jessica studied her. "It is important?"

"Very." Sierra didn't know if the loss of life would motivate the Keeper. But it was important. To Sierra. To all those dark haired, fair skinned women.

The Keeper nodded. "I can."

"Email okay?"

"Just verbalize them. I have room, still," Jessica said, tapping her head. A clump of white hair loosened and fell to the marble floor.

Eww. Sierra rattled off the list. Her memory wasn't that of a Keeper, trained to remember the details of hundreds of worlds, but she knew her data.

"I have them. Email?"

"I have room," Sierra said. Twenty-four worlds, who knew how many agents per world. "But email me a back up."

Jessica recited the list of names.

Five were new to Sierra, and she tucked them away at the back of her brain for just in case, in the future, because no data was ever wasted—but none of them matched more than a couple of the worlds and times. None of them was her murderer.

But, of the three that Sierra had targeted...only one had visited every single world, at the correct time.

Field Agent Kieran Jackson.

Her classmate.

"Thank you," Sierra whispered.

Jessica nodded serenely. "You have the knowledge you sought."

"I do."

"Peace, child."

Peace? Not yet. But there would be.

SIERRA'S BRAIN skidded and bounced. Office. She had to compile the data. Complete her analysis. Create her report. Who could she send it to? Her supervisor wasn't a man of action. She needed someone to take her seriously, and act swiftly. She needed her computer. Her safe space. She threw open her office door, welcoming the lavender-scented mustiness, the reflective glare of the bank of monitors in the dark room, and shut the door behind her.

"Monitors on," she said, and her monitors sputtered to life, scrolling the feeds of dozens of worlds, illuminating the tiny room.

Illuminating Kieran.

"Hi, Sierra." His teeth were bright in the light from the monitors. He leaned against her desk, one hand on the closed lid of her laptop.

He was the male version of Sadie, the ideal of a male field agent. Capable of dealing with any physical situation, whether it was a fight or a natural disaster. Of completing any variety of mission, with only his body and wits to rely upon.

Of ripping apart innocent women, for his debased pleasure.

She detested him.

"Hi, Kieran. How are you?" she said. He was touching her laptop.

He tracked her gaze, stroked the laptop lid. "I'm doing just dandy, Sierra. You?"

"I'll be fine, once you're gone."

"I doubt that. Love your hair, by the way. Prettiest thing about you. You're such a sad ugly troll, living in your cave down here. Except that hair. That's nice." He straightened. "Come here, Sierra, you nosy little troll. If you don't scream, I'll make it quick. Skip, skip on over here."

Did he know that she'd worked with Sadie? With Jessica?

"I don't want to die," she said meekly. Troll? She wasn't a troll. Fuck him.

But even more importantly, she had to protect the others.

She shuffled forward one step. Two. The edge of her desk. She was within his reach, if he wanted to grab; but he seemed to enjoy her fear, her walking to her own death.

She swept her left foot under the desk. There.

The remnants of her coffee cup.

She dropped to her knees and grabbed the biggest shard, not caring that it sliced into her palm as she clenched it—

—and stabbed with all her weight and force and desperation at his muscled torso, ripping up then stabbing and slashing at his neck—

—as he screamed in fury and pain until his voice was swallowed by a wet moist gurgle—

—and the stench of loosened bowels that meant no number of lavender candles would do the trick to freshen her office.

He had collapsed across her laptop.

She shoved him off the laptop, his body crumpling to the floor.

She wiped at her laptop. She couldn't get the blood off. It wouldn't come off. It just coated her hands.

She sank to the floor, next to him, and cried.

SIERRA STOOD at attention at Director Jason Osaka's desk. She'd never even dreamed she'd someday meet the Director. She hadn't ever wanted to.

His wood-paneled office with the heavy Mission furniture, California Impressionist paintings, and antique rifles and sabers was meant to impress. His close-cropped iron colored hair, ramrod bearing, and neatly pressed uniform over a muscular physique completed the picture.

She wasn't impressed.

Trappings, all of it.

He motioned for Sierra to sit.

"I know you've already been debriefed. I just wanted to talk to you. See how you're doing. Thank you for your quick action."

"I should never have been in that position," she said. "You run us through so many medical, physical, and psychological tests, you should have known Kieran was a sociopath, with the potential to do what he did. Even if you chose to not expel him from the program, because there are so few of us that can Gate, you should have watched him. But you didn't. And women died. Their deaths *matter*, and it's your fault."

"Right now," he said evenly, "you're a hero. But that can change."

"I'm sure it will," Sierra said. "But until you decide to fire me, I'm going to keep doing my job. And I'm going to do my best to make sure nothing like this happens again."

She stood up. "And I'm going to make sure it's not happened before. I'm going to dig up any skeletons I find. I'm willing to work with you, Director. As long as you will work with me.

"But people need to be held accountable. And I can't let that go. If there needs to be someone to speak for the other worlds, to keep us honest, well. I'm it.

"I'm it."

THE EMBRACE OF THE GATE

Pulsing streaks of orange marred the jet black shimmer of the Gate filling the center of the marble-floored transit room.

The streaks flared into flames, and the gate popped and spat like a grease fire. The room stank like burning two day old skunk road kill.

Jessica took one look at the junior Gate Keeper, fighting to keep control of the Gate, his face rigid. His eyebrows were scorched where the Gate had scored him. A thin line of spittle hung from his lower lip.

He looked so *young*. She sighed.

Two other junior Keepers, both women, huddled just outside the doorway. The younger woman had fetched Jessica from her quarters when the Gate went bad.

Jessica had been meditating, preparing for her duties as Keeper that evening. She'd just finished her lunch of chicken broth and plain bread, all her energy-depleted body could keep down, and had left orders to be disturbed only in case of an emergency.

This counted.

The lives of the Field Agents on the other side of the Gate depended on her, now.

"World?" she asked, her voice raspy with disuse. She cleared her throat. "What world, child?"

"Alpha Two Charlie," the older female Keeper said.

At least someone had their wits about them.

Alpha Two Charlie was a near copy of Earth Prime, only a couple details to focus on to bring the Gate into being.

An easy Gate. Not like the one she'd have to create for this evening's mission, for Zebra Nine Golf.

Yet the young man trembled with the stress of trying to contain the Gate.

A Gate *should* look like a swath of glittering jet bisecting the transit room.

And Gates, healthy Gates, were silent. Serene.

Not on fire, crackling and snapping.

What had the boy *done*?

Jessica reached for the Gate, thin hands beckoning. *Come to momma.*

A whip of flame snapped at her hand. She didn't flinch.

You know better, she chided. *Come on.* Los Angeles, the canals of Venice re-engineered so that the daily tides flushed them clean. Just a small change, in the big picture. Her hands stroked the air, creating currents that soothed the Gate, as her memory focused on the canals, the ocean, the brine heavy on the air.

Jessssica?

She knew that voice.

Her old teacher, long absorbed into the Gates.

Not yet, she told the Gate.

All the Gates now asked her to join them. And she always told them no.

"Come closer," she said to the two female Keepers. "Observe. Then repeat my movements. Focus on your chosen details of Alpha Two Charlie. Can you feel the Gate responding?"

The two younger Keepers complied, their faces tense, their movements jerky.

They would learn.

The flames subsided, and the angry orange dulled to peach, then pale violet, then indigo, til it darkened to black. The stench dissipated, though Jessica figured she'd have to wash her hair as soon as she returned to her quarters unless she wanted to smell like burning skunk for the next day.

If she had the energy.

Two young male field agents, dressed in jeans and t-shirts rather than the typical Prime-side uniform of khakis and sage green collared shirts, stumbled through the gate into the transit room. The jeans and t-shirts bore char marks.

Singed, but safe.

The junior keeper in charge of the Gate collapsed.

"Welcome home," Jessica said to the field agents. "I hope your mission was a success.

"And you two—get your fellow Keeper to the infirmary." She nodded to the junior Keepers. "I'll be back later this evening for my shift."

Jessica made it halfway to her quarters before her foot caught on the low pile of the industrial carpet of the hallway. She stumbled, bruising her shoulder against the smooth white wall, before catching herself.

No one had seen her. Her gaze flicked to a shiny black half-sphere affixed to the ceiling.

Well, no one in person saw her. And security couldn't monitor every camera feed.

Another bowl of broth. That would tide her through the evening's work.

It had to.

SHE'D DRANK HALF a mug of honey-sweetened Earl Gray before Director Jason Osaka summoned her. She hadn't even had the chance to heat some broth.

The sugar got her to his office, at least.

The wood paneled room, a cliché of upper level masculine bureaucracy with its old heavy oak furniture and faded Persian carpet, was pleasantly warm. She suspected he'd done that for her. But he'd never admit it.

The Director of the Bureau of Interworld Stabilization, or BIS, a no-nonsense middle-aged man, suited the masculine office decor. The physical ideal of a field agent with his muscular physique and ramrod straight posture, he still trained with the BIS recruits, going on group runs and completing the various obstacle courses.

Keepers were exempt from such training after graduation. The Gates themselves took too much energy.

Someday, soon, she would be absorbed into the Gates. She wouldn't be able to keep saying no. She didn't know what would happen next. Sometimes, like today, when she opened Gates, she thought she heard the voices of long-gone Keepers who had trained her, like the echoes of the different worlds. Sometimes, it was just a voice. The Gate itself? Who knew.

Their words, though still unintelligible, now sounded like they were just next door.

As close as Alpha Two Charlie.

She no longer feared her ending.

"Good evening, Director Osaka," Jessica said.

"Sit, Jessica," Osaka said. He opened a folder labeled JESSICA MORAINE. Her hard copy personnel file. All personnel files were hard copy, not digitized, after an incident with data mining from Alpha Two Alpha.

"I'd rather not." Her knees ached too much when she stood back up.

He didn't insist. Just looked at her, his expression bland.

She knew what he saw. A ghost of a woman, with hardly enough flesh to cover her bones.

"Good job handling those three earlier today. For getting Agents Royka and Lewis back safely. Their mission was critical."

She didn't care about the particulars. Field agents went to the various worlds, completed their assigned missions to keep bad things from echoing back to Prime, and returned.

Her job was the Gate. Giving the agents a means to get to and from those worlds.

"I shouldn't have had to intervene."

"No," he agreed. "You shouldn't have. How old are you, Jessica?"

"Forty years, three months, and two days." He knew her age. It was in her file. What was his point?

"Younger than me. You look twenty years older," he commented drily.

"I don't see how that has any bearing on my performance."

"It doesn't. Except I don't know how much longer you can do your job."

"I won't fail during a Gate." No Gate would fail her.

He leaned back, hands clasped behind his head.

"You've taught before."

"I didn't enjoy it." He *couldn't*. He couldn't take her from the Gates.

"I'm taking you off Gate duty as of now. There's a wild Gate in Santa Fe that's cycling. I want you to investigate and report back to me. After that, we can discuss your career path." He leaned forward, thick hands now flat on the desk. "You are the most experienced Keeper we have. I'm not losing that experience to the Gates. Not now.

"Not until you get your successors properly trained, at least."

"I—"

"Not up for discussion. Keeper Desoto will take your assignment for tonight. Report to Logistics ASAP. Your flight leaves in two hours from LAX. Dismissed, Keeper Moraine."

BIS HAD CHARTERED a sleek private jet that boasted a bar, a shower, and a king sized bed in the rear of the jet.

"Borrowed from DEA," the pilot, a tiny gray-haired woman, said as Jessica boarded and gawked. "Belonged to some dead drug lord. Enjoy. Take a nap if you'd like, once we get airborne. Flight time is about two hours."

"Thanks," Jessica said. "But I have homework." She settled into her seat, a plush saddle tan leather recliner.

Director Osaka had sent over a packet of notes on the wild Gate for her to review before arriving in Santa Fe. She needed to go over it.

The cabin smelled clean, except for the bit of skunk that Jessica hadn't had time to wash out of her hair. The small air jets in the ceiling blew in the outside air for the time being. Balmy late winter Los Angeles, with a hint of brine from the nearby ocean. She shivered, then huddled in her seat to read.

Wild Gates popped up sporadically. Alien abductions? Bigfoot sightings? Fairies stealing humans? Usually due to wild Gates.

Most wild Gates appeared for a few hours, then disappeared. This one, located in an abandoned adobe homestead on a couple of acres in the foothills of the Sangre de Cristo Mountains, had appeared a week ago. The Albuquerque field office, which served all of New Mexico, had assigned personnel to guard the Gate—or rather, to keep anyone going through it. Nominally the property was private, but the field office agent in charge, or AIC, Alex Morales, worried someone hiking might stumble upon it.

Agent Lori Buck slid into the seat facing Jessica.

"Wow! This is pretty amazing." Buck bounced in the seat, then snugged her seat belt across her lap. "Super comfy. I've never been in a plane like this. Have you?"

Director Osaka had assigned Jessica an assistant: Field Agent Lori Buck, just a year out from graduation, with her khaki trousers and sage green shirt neatly pressed, and her beach blond hair in a tight French braid.

"Ooh, you're shivering. Let me find you a blanket." Buck unfastened her seat belt and bounced up. She came back in a less than a minute. "An alpaca blend throw. This should work!"

Young and green and bright eyed and bushy-tailed. But Buck

could be useful, to carry Jessica's luggage. Or so Director Osaka had said, in response to Jessica's outraged call when she first encountered Buck at Logistics.

"After we get going, Director Osaka said I was to make sure you ate. He had me pick up some nutrient shakes for you."

Was the man *trying* to goad her into the embrace of a Gate before her time?

"I'm not hungry."

"Director Osaka said you'd say that. But that I had to make sure you eat."

The jet took off. Quiet. She could barely here the thrum of the jets.

Much quieter than her unwelcome assistant.

"I will dump it over your head if you force the issue."

"He said you'd say that too. And that I was to ignore it." Her pansy blue eyes darkened. "Keeper Moraine, let me do my job. I know you don't think we have much—or anything—in common. But I bet I take doing a good job as seriously as you do."

Jessica sighed. "Fine. Pass one over."

Buck opened a small soft-sided cooler and withdrew a fuchsia-colored enameled insulated bottle with a built-in straw.

"I had the cafeteria make you up a couple fresh. The second will keep til tomorrow for breakfast once I get it into a fridge. Berries, greens, goat yogurt, soy protein. An electrolyte and vitamin supplement, too, but I figured the berries would hide the taste." She watched anxiously as Jessica sipped it.

"It's good," Jessica admitted. Her stomach roiled, but she'd keep the smoothie down, no matter what.

"Director Osaka said you'd need these, too," Buck said, fishing out a small orange pill vial. "Two at each meal. Since you're not much used to solid food."

A smoothie counted as solid? Jessica shook out two tablets. Antacids.

To be fair, she didn't know the last time she'd eaten anything besides broth, tea, and plain white bread. She chewed the tablets. Her stomach did settle.

A bit.

Maybe this wouldn't be so bad.

BUCK GRABBED Jessica's carryon as well as her own, plus the small cooler. AIC Morales met them at the Santa Fe regional airport in his own private vehicle, an aging minivan crowded with kid's toys and car seats and smelling like old orange juice and sour milk.

"The Director sprung for a swanky rental house near the site," he said. "Hop in. It's not too long of a drive. Do you need to stop anywhere for anything?"

"Nope," Buck said. "Keeper Moraine needs a good night's sleep, then we'll be raring to go in the morning."

Jessica glared at her. Did she look *that* frail?

Apparently so, because AIC Morales didn't even question Buck's statement.

"Sorry for the mess," he said as they climbed in, Buck in the middle bank of seats, Jessica in the passenger's seat.

"I have two little brothers," said Buck. "I'm used to it."

The two chatted throughout the drive about the wild Gate. Nothing that Jessica hadn't read in the report. She wanted to make her own assessment, anyways.

The moon had set, and the night sky was velvety despite the light pollution from Santa Fe. They drove east, away from the city and up into the foothills, and the sky darkened. The road surface changed from asphalt to hard-packed dirt, mounds of snow pushed to the sides, before they reached the rental, a sprawling adobe-style ranchette surrounded by junipers and prickly pear.

"Nice," commented Buck.

New Mexico was so very different than Playa del Rey, with its mix of wetlands and shrubs, where BIS was headquartered. Jessica hadn't left the Los Angeles area since earning her position as a senior Keeper, fifteen years prior.

The Gates had been all she needed.

"We'll get you set up with a four wheel rental tomorrow. I don't think you'll need four wheel drive, but I'd rather be prepared," Morales said. "If it snows, you'll want it. Entry code for the house is 9731. It's stocked with breakfast fixings. I'll pick you up tomorrow at nine a.m."

"Sounds good," Jessica said. "Thank you."

Buck assigned Jessica the master suite, after poking her head into the various bedrooms.

"This is yours," Buck said, satisfied. "Want me to unpack for you, while you take a shower?"

The suite was three times the size of her quarters at BIS. A king-sized pine canopy bed filled the front half of the room. Beyond it was a sitting area with two leather armchairs, facing a white-plastered kiva fireplace. A turquoise painted desk was arranged under the bank of windows that faced the peaks of the Sangre de Cristo mountains. The room smelled like sage and pinon.

"That would be nice. Really nice," Jessica said. "Thank you."

She wouldn't get used to this. She wouldn't.

A Keeper's life was spartan. All she needed was the Gates, the infinite expanse between worlds. Eternity.

But the shower with nozzles that sprayed her from three different directions with hot water...the thick warm robe that almost wrapped around her twice, and the shearling slippers...and the huge firm bed, with its velvet duvet and down comforter....

Nothing said she couldn't enjoy it for the time being. She nestled under the comforter. It was okay that she enjoyed it.

It really was.

JESSICA SLEPT UNTIL EIGHT, the squawk of a jay waking her. She sat up and looked out the window. Her breath fogged the air, and she kept the comforter tucked under her chin. A huge heavyset deer was nibbling on the tall dry grass on the other side of the hard packed dirt driveway, the morning sunlight sparking gold on its dusty hide.

He looked up at her, his eyes dark as a Gate, then bent his head down again to grab another wad of grass.

She hadn't dreamed.

It was the first time in fifteen years she hadn't dreamed.

She prodded at the idea like a sore tooth. Scrap that. Like a sore tooth that had been fixed, the ache just a phantom.

She had slept like a rock.

It was wonderful.

Someone knocked on her bedroom door. The deer bounded away, its tail flicking over its white butt.

"Are you up, Jessica? I'm fixing some scrambled eggs and coffee. And there's your shake, too." Buck. Obviously a morning person.

"I'm awake. Um, is there heat?"

"It's warm out here. I'll check the vents in your room after breakfast."

"Thanks. Did you see the deer?"

"It's an elk!"

Jessica laughed. "I thought it was a big fat deer."

She shrugged on the robe and stuck her feet into the slippers. That would do until Buck got her room warmed up. She assumed that Buck, or someone in Logistics, had packed her a couple sets of uniforms. Keepers usually wore light wool robes, not the regular uniforms, but that wouldn't work for a field assignment.

The hallway was a good twenty degrees warmer than her room. She shut the bedroom door behind her, then padded to the main room, the soles of her slippers sinking into the thick pile of the hallway carpet.

The rich smell of fresh eggs, onions, and peppers greeted her.

The living area was open concept, with the kitchen and island roughly taking the western third of the room, with a view towards Santa Fe below. A long pine dining table filled the center, extending almost to where the hallway opened to the great room. The sitting area, with two leather loveseats and two velvet armchairs, looked out to the east at the Sangre de Cristos mountains.

The far side of the dining room, and both corners of the sitting area, had wood-burning kiva fireplaces, all unlit, but with wood stacked and ready to light.

Thick wool carpets cushioned the Saltillo tile floors under the dining room table and the sofas.

It was so luxurious. So unlike anything she'd ever known.

"I'm making your eggs separate from the vege," Buck said. She wore a pink gingham cotton apron over her crisp BIS uniform. "Not sure if your stomach can take the heat of the peppers yet. But boy, you have something to look forward to. Coffee?"

"Yes, please." Jessica hadn't had coffee in years. She felt daring. "Cream?"

"There's both half and half and heavy cream."

"Cream." She could be decadent. It wasn't like she couldn't afford the calories.

"Sit! I'll bring it to you."

Jessica let Buck pull out her chair, then tuck her closer to the table. Buck brought Jessica coffee in a sturdy porcelain diner mug, with a small carafe of cream on the side, then went back for the smoothie and a plate of scrambled eggs.

Buck carried back the bowls of peppers and onions and her own plate of scrambled eggs, then plopped across from Jessica. "Help yourself to the peppers and onions," she said. "Just be careful, the peppers really are hot."

Jessica dug into the eggs. Buck had cooked them in butter. Delicious. She waited for her stomach to rebel, but nothing happened. Coffee. Cream. A spoonful of onions, and the tiniest taste of peppers.

"Oh, gosh, you weren't kidding," Jessica gasped. "Hot, hot, hot!"

"Smoothie! The yogurt will help with the heat." Buck grinned. "But they're good, right?"

"Oh yes," Jessica said, after she quaffed half the smoothie. "But I think that was enough for now."

She'd eaten more than she usually ate in a week.

"Okay, you get ready, I'll clean up. I can blend up a smoothie for you for later, if you'd like." Buck watched her closely. "You know, like hobbits. Second breakfast."

"I can't promise I have any room for it," Jessica said.

"That's what the cooler is for. It'll keep." Buck smiled. "Thanks, Jessica. I appreciate how hard you're trying."

Jessica shook her head. "You're being great. I'm sorry if I was horrible yesterday."

"Nah. You're fine," Buck said. "Everyone knows Keepers are a bit odd, anyways."

Jessica laughed. "I guess we are, sometimes."

LOGISTICS HADN'T PACKED uniforms for her. Rather, they'd included a selection of thermal underwear, both flannel-lined and unlined jeans, several cozy wool sweaters, a wool parka, and a puffy down jacket.

The only thing regulation was the thick soled hiking boots.

Jessica didn't think the cashmere-blend socks were standard.

She marveled at the softness of the underwear. Her frame was so sparse she had no need of a bra; the snug undershirt kept the wool sweater from making her itchy. Not that she thought the wool itchy. It too was amazingly soft, soft as a bunny. She checked the label. Wool and angora. It *was* bunny.

Buck knocked as she was tugging the laces tight on her boots. "Got the air figured out," she said cheerfully. "It should be toasty well before we get back tonight. And we can always light a fire."

"Sounds wonderful," Jessica said. "Are you always this nice?"

Buck smiled, her blue eyes darkening. "Yep."

A horn honked.

"Time to work," Jessica said. Her belly clenched—not in discomfort, but in...excitement? Yes. She was excited to see this wild Gate. To test it. To test herself against it.

Jessica hadn't felt this eager about anything in years.

~

AIC Morales was driving his minivan. Agent Gertz, one of the agents on duty for guarding the gate, drove the rental, a four-wheel drive black sport utility vehicle. He tossed the keys to Buck.

"Long time no see, Lori. She's all yours," he said to Buck, then turned to Jessica. "Care if I ride with you, ma'am? Can't stand all the kid stuff in Morale's vehicle. Nothing against kids. It just smells."

"Gertz, you're just a wimp," called Morales.

"That's fine," Jessica said to Gertz. "I'd like to talk to you about the Gate, anyways."

Buck followed Morales to the site, down several increasingly bumpy dirt roads. The last was unplowed, a mix of melting snow and ice. Their vehicle handled the snow just fine, unlike Morale's minivan, fishtailing ahead of them on the slick irregular surface.

Gertz didn't really have any input beyond what she'd read in Morale's report. The Gate was quiet, a silent swath of black in one corner of the roofless adobe shell, all that remained of the former homestead. Nothing came through from the other side. They didn't go through, because they didn't have a Keeper to ensure they could get back. Yes, if she would anchor the Gate, Gertz was willing to go through and try to learn if it was a new, unexplored world. Yes, he understood the risk, as did Miller, the second agent guarding the gate. She was willing to go through it with Gertz.

"You understand I may not be able to keep it open. Or re-open it, if it closes."

Gertz shrugged. "That's a risk no matter what. From what I hear, from other Keepers, you're the best Keeper working right now. I'd rather Gate somewhere new, with you, than to an adjacent world with some untried kid."

"Well, it wouldn't be today. Or even the next day. I'd have to study its world. Learn it. Love it. I can't rush that." That tingle again, in her stomach. When was the last time she'd studied a new world?

Too long.

The snow crunched under her boots as she walked to the adobe, Buck steadying her with a hand on Jessica's elbow.

She squinted towards the corner.

The Gate was *beautiful.* It stretched a good ten feet across, bigger than any wild Gate she'd ever read about, let alone seen. Galaxies spun across its darkness. She could feel the world beyond. A virgin world, full of elk and jays and rattlesnakes and hawks. Juniper and pinon. Snow glinting on the peaks, a wash of crimson in the sunrise.

Jesssssica. A happy sigh. It loved her, and she loved it.

And it wanted her separate. Unique. Not absorbed into itself.

She reached to the Gate, stroking the nebulous cool sheen. It licked at her fingertips, as curious as a kitten. The rough scrape drew pinpoints of blood.

It tasted her. Then paused. Evaluated.

Then, with a deep sorrow, it withdrew.

"Don't go!" She leapt for the shrinking swath of swirling darkness.

All her adult life, she had known she would go into a Gate, and never return. And now this Gate...it didn't want to take. It wanted to share.

She fell, bashing her knees against the frozen ground, scraping her palms bloody.

Too physically weak.

Too weak, agreed the Gate. It showed her the high desert. Bighorn sheep. A rushing river.

She wanted to wail. To beg.

But she wouldn't. She never had, and she never would.

Live, it said. *Grow strong. Find me then. But LIVE.*

The Gate disappeared.

～

BUCK DREW a bubble bath for Jessica. She helped Jessica undress, helped her lower her frail body into the hot water. The water stung Jessica's torn palms. She welcomed the pain.

"I'll bring you some hot chocolate." Buck popped up to her feet. "Whipped cream?"

Jessica closed her eyes, sunk into the water up to her chin. "Gertz. He said long time no see. I thought you graduated only last year."

"I thought you'd missed that."

"I'm a Keeper. I'm trained to notice everything. Though I've not been doing a great job of it, this trip."

Buck sighed. "You look old for your age. I look young. Dr Lori Buck, clinical psychologist. Nice to meet you, Jessica Moraine."

"This was a set up. Coming to study this Gate. All this luxury. Everything."

"No. You need to get healthy. Jessica, your duties were killing you. And Director Osaka knows he can't afford to lose you. Those Keepers screwing up Alpha Two Charlie was real. He needs you to teach the baby Keepers how to handle the Gates."

Buck paused.

"And this wild Gate? Serendipity. Osaka would have found something, some excuse, to get you out of BIS HQ. The other stuff is the cherry on top. So enjoy it. And, yes, this Gate was perfect for you. A Gate that didn't want to, frankly, *eat* you. A Gate that wanted to partner with you. I didn't know it would leave you. We've had other Keepers studying it. I thought it would stay," said Buck.

"You were so nice to me. Just because it's your job." Gah. That sounded so whiny.

"Jessica, believe me, you are an amazing woman. Driven. More than a bit scary. But I like you. I want to help you. And I was telling you the truth. I want to do my job just as well as you do yours." She shrugged. "That's part of me. Just like it's part of you. Now. Whipped cream?"

"Yes, please." Jessica waited until she couldn't hear Buck's footsteps, then closed her eyes, held her breath, and immersed herself.

She held her breath til her chest ached. Til she almost sucked in water.

She sat up, gasping.

It wasn't her time. Not yet.

She would get healthy. And then she would choose. She might teach. She might seek this gate. She might seek her long gone teachers.

But it would be her choice.

Hers.

APPENDIX
WORLDS MENTIONED IN GATES OF WONDER

The closer a world is to Prime, the closer its alphanumeric designation.

Alpha Two Charlie: A near copy of Prime. Venice Beach-A2C is a bit different than Venice Beach in Prime. The canals have been re-engineered so that the daily tides flush them clean. It should be an easy world for newbie Gate Keepers to access. *The Embrace of the Gate*

Alpha Six Delta: Has a biome 95.98% the same as Earth Prime. The world is fully catalogued. Los Angeles-A6D is a small farming town. *The Cry of the Coyote*

Alpha Eleven Alpha: A world that was more technologically advanced than Prime. Singularity. Izzy wonders—is this world, A11A, the true Prime? *Agent Izzy Austin and the Main Brain Mainframe*

Charlie One Theta: A nice mix of Prime-similar tech and, for want of a better word, magic. Los Angeles-C1T is recognizably Los Angeles: big and sprawling and crowded. Just with a touch of magic. *An Overdose of Espresso*

Delta Nine Omega: Bigger than Los Angeles, Earth Prime. Fifty percent more people crowded into the basin, if Sierra's memory is correct. A hotbed of violence. *Skip Skip You're It*

Romeo One Foxtrot: Los Angeles-R1F is a sleepy port town. Murders are uncommon, the police staff not as practiced as that of Delta Nine Omega. *Skip Skip You're It*

Zebra Nine Golf: Very very far away from Prime! Jessica doesn't say much about this world, Z9G. *The Embrace of the Gate*

A Note on Wild Gates: Wild Gates can go anywhere and show up anywhere. Fairyland? Alien abduction? These rumors and legends come from Wild Gates.

And of course, if BIS isn't in control of the Gate, they consider it wild.

The Embrace of the Gate; An Overdose of Espresso

ABOUT THE AUTHOR

Since graduating from West Point, Stephannie Tallent has served in the Army as a Military Intelligence officer during Desert Storm, gotten a Zoology degree, went to vet school, worked as a small animal veterinarian, and designed and published knitting patterns and books.

Throughout all that she's always wanted to be a writer, and she's finally put all her type A, soft-spoken, invisible middle-aged woman focus on that goal, writing everything from fantasy to science fiction, mysteries and romance.

She has sold stories to **Pulphouse Magazine** and the **WMG Holiday Spectacular.**

www.stephannietallent.com

Sign up for my newsletter!
https://www.stephannietallent.com/subscribe/

ALSO BY STEPHANNIE TALLENT

Short Story Collections

Gates of Wonder

The Chronicles of Dinah Lee Wright Vol 1

The Chronicles of Dinah Lee Wright Vol 2

Gratitude of the Ocean: Jolene Tomberlin Series

The Serpent in the Shallows: Jolene Tomberlin Series

The Monkey's Journal

The Kaleidoscope Jaguars of the Jungles of Mexicatl

The Mermaid of Ellis Prime

The Alchemy of Science and Mystery

One Plus One Equals More (mystery/crime)

A Snowman Made of Sand (romance)

KnitWitch (fantasy and knitting patterns)